Pirate Patch

and the

Five-minute Fortune

In which the triumphant Pirate Patch and his capable crew find a fortune - then lose it to their old enemies. But that's only half the story!

For Reuben
R.I.

For Lowen
N.R.

Reading Consultant: Prue Goodwin, Lecturer in Literacy and
Children's Books at the University of Reading

ORCHARD BOOKS
338 Euston Road, London NW1 3BH
Orchard Books Australia
Hachette Children's Books
Level 17/207 Kent Street, Sydney NSW 2000

First published by Orchard Books in 2009

Text © Rose Impey 2009
Illustrations © Nathan Reed 2009

A CIP catalogue record for this book is available from the British Library

ISBN 978 1 84362 980 1 (hardback)
ISBN 978 1 84362 988 7 (paperback)

1 3 5 7 9 10 8 6 4 2
Printed in China

Orchard Books is a division of Hachette Children's Books,
an Hachette Livre UK company.
www.hachettelivre.co.uk

Pirate Patch

and the

Five-minute Fortune

ROSE IMPEY · NATHAN REED

ORCHARD BOOKS

It was definitely their lucky day.
Patch and his *capable* crew had
found buried treasure, at last!

As they sailed home in *The Little Pearl*, Patch, Peg and Portside dreamed of all the things the treasure would buy them.

They were so busy
celebrating, even Pierre,
the lookout, was off duty.

Which is how their two old enemies – the *villainous* Bones and Jones – managed to sneak onto their ship . . .

. . . and capture them all!

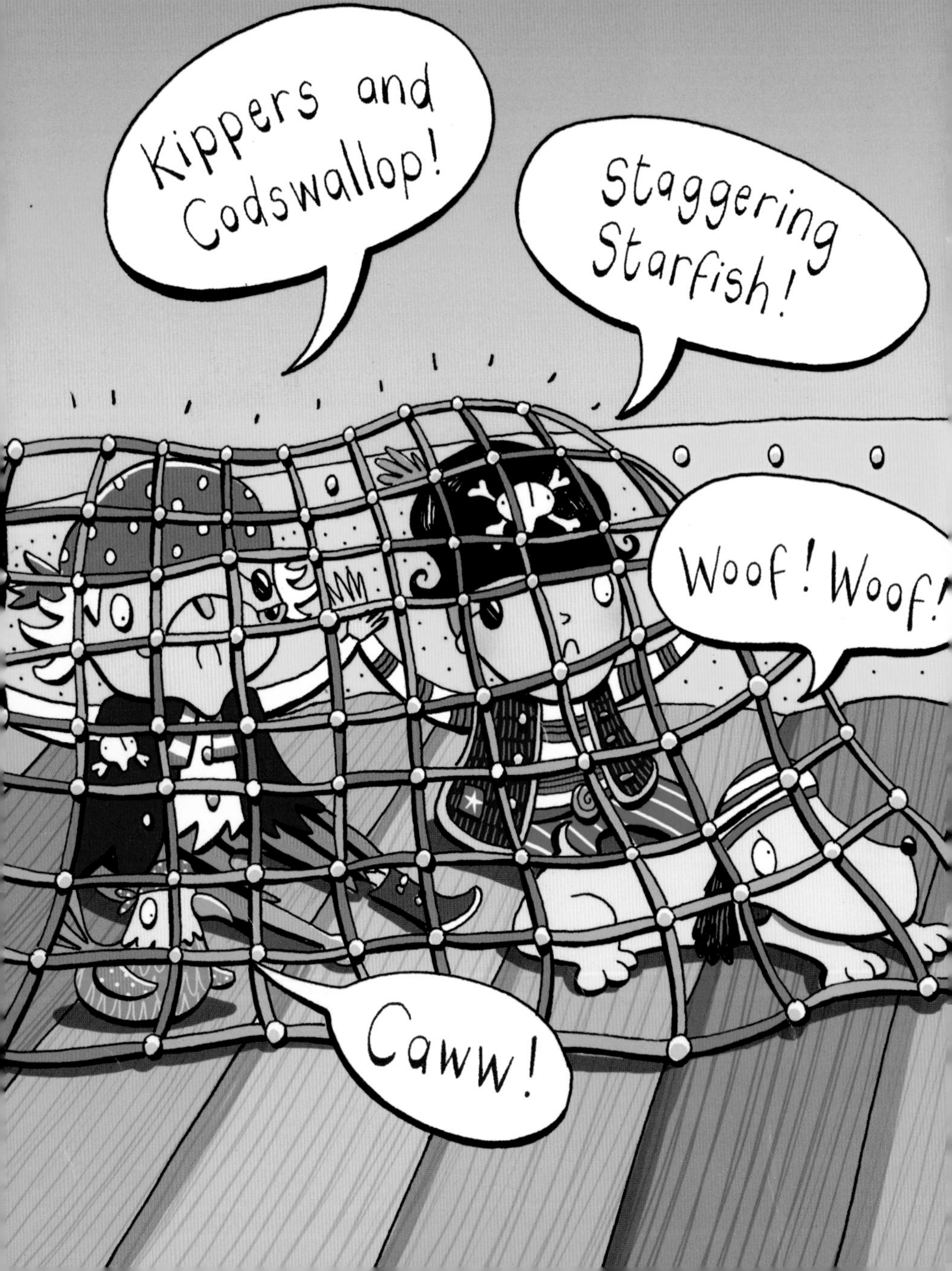

Bones and Jones took Patch
and his crew back to their ship:
The Black Bonnet. And they took
the treasure too!

The two villains put Patch and
Peg in chains and threw the
whole crew in the hold.

Patch wondered how they would ever escape. Even Portside, the cleverest sea dog ever to sail the seven seas, couldn't chew through chains!

Suddenly there was a
terrible noise overhead.

15

Patch could hear shouting
and swords clashing.
It sounded as if a battle
was going on above deck.

Patch would have liked to join in.
But in no time the battle was over.
Then the hold opened and through
it fell . . .

. . . Bones and Jones!

17

The scurvy pair were already arguing about whose fault it was. Patch told them to stop arguing and tell him what had happened!

"A *huge* gang of pirates came out of nowhere," said Bones.

"How huge?" asked Patch.

"At least ten!" said Bones.

"More like *twenty*!" argued Jones.

Patch didn't really trust those two villains. But he knew he had to make a deal with them.

"Give us the key first," he told Bones and Jones. "Then we'll untie you."

Bones and Jones didn't like that plan at all.
But after a lot of arguing, they agreed to make a deal – just this once!

"Now let's get our ship back," said Bones. "Follow me!"

"No, follow me!" said Jones.

"*I'm* the captain!" Patch told them, firmly. "Follow me!"

Everyone lined up behind Patch, who bravely lifted the hold and peeped out.

But there was no *huge* gang of pirates waiting for them. And no treasure either!

Bones and Jones were furious.
"Those pesky pirates took our
treasure," they complained.
"*Our* treasure," Patch
reminded them.

For a moment it looked as if
the scurvy pair had forgotten
they were all on the same side.
But Patch and Peg soon
reminded them.

Back on *The Little Pearl*, Patch quickly set sail. He needed to be home before Mum and Dad found him missing.

Patch had finally found his fortune and five minutes later he'd lost it. But at least Bones and Jones hadn't got it! So who had, he wondered?

Later, when Mum and Dad
came home, Patch found out . . .
"Look at these," said Mum. "Have
you ever seen such jewels before?"

Patch and Peg certainly had.
But they shook their heads
and wisely said . . . nothing.

★ Pirate Patch ★

Rose Impey   Nathan Reed

All priced at £8.99

Orchard Colour Crunchies are available from all good bookshops,
or can be ordered direct from the publisher:
Orchard Books, PO BOX 29, Douglas IM99 1BQ
Credit card orders please telephone 01624 836000
or fax 01624 837033 or visit our internet site: www.orchardbooks.co.uk
or e-mail: bookshop@enterprise.net for details.

To order please quote title, author and ISBN
and your full name and address.
Cheques and postal orders should be made payable to 'Bookpost plc.'
Postage and packing is FREE within the UK
(overseas customers should add £2.00 per book).

Prices and availability are subject to change.